I0671160

ScavengeReaper

Written by

Stacy Cox   StaceMeister0

Introducing active contribution and participation.

ISBN 978-0-359-94377-7

To Lyric & Londyn.

MATURE CONTENT

ScavengeReaper is not suitable for minors. Content includes vulgar language, nudity, and violence.

NOTICE

THE NAMES, DATES, AND EVENTS IN THIS STORY ARE 100% FICTITIOUS AND RANDOMLY GENERATED FOR ENTERTAINMENT PURPOSES. ANY SIMILAR ENTITIES ARE COMPLETELY COINCIDENTAL.

Table Of Contents

Special Thanks

*With **ScavengeReaper**, I wanted to conduct an experiment, where I would have active participation and social commentary from my community of supporters.*

I presented an activity to a handful of people, where I asked them to think of an activity that is unethical, unorthodox, unlawful, and extreme. Unbeknownst to them, the participants would construct their own characters and path in this story.

*I would like to acknowledge the following people for their amazing contributions and participation in **ScavengeReaper**.*

Selina Dickenson

Dakota Dodge

Jerry Ramsey

Marcus Brown

Dave Taylor

David Roslan

Paul Dulski of *Everything Horror Podcasts.* Follow Paul and Everything Horror Podcasts:

Official Site: https://ehpodcasts.com/

Twitch: http://www.twitch.tv/ehpodcasts

YouTube: https://www.youtube.com/EHPodcasts

Facebook: @EHPodcasts

Twitter: @EHPodcasts

Instagram: @ehpodcasts

Ferass Doleh (a.k.a. Kane) of *Everything Comics!*
Follow Ferass and Everything Comics!

Facebook:
https://www.facebook.com/groups/2652636003
10683/

Sacrifice

By Kane Doleh

You a broken man;

Has been chosen

To become a king.

All you have to do

To say the word;

"I sacrifice."

You will have the power of darkness.

You will become a dark lord among us.

You will feel no pain.

You will not know sorrow.

You will not know struggle.

For you will be the newest dark lord.

Will you utter the words?

Will you suffer the same fate as your kinsman?

"I SACRIFICE!"

He has said the words.

Let the feast begin.

As our newest kinsman is reborn.

ScavengeReaper

Where It All Began

History In The Making

30 years ago...

Evelyn and Eryn flee from their home. They lost their parents several months ago, and they soon discovered the cause of their deaths.

♟

6 months before...

Valerie and Don struggle against their restraints as they try to free themselves from the binds that hold them. They express looks of terror as they are surrounded by the cult of Satanists that prepare them to be sacrificed to the dark Lord.

Don lets out a soul-stricken scream as the contraction begins to pull his arms and legs in opposite directions, ripping his limbs apart.

Valerie becomes wide-eyed as she notices the contraction above her. A large screwdriver-type contraction. It powers on and eases toward her. She squeals as the sharp, ridged edges of the screw pierces her chest.

☠

6 months later...

Evelyn screams and struggles as she is grabbed by her uncle, Mitchell. The same person who sacrificed their parents to a group of Satanists. Mitchell screams and drops Evelyn to the floor.

Evelyn scurries from his grip but stops as Mitchell drops to the floor. She sighs in relief as she realizes her brother, Eryn came to her rescue, stabbing Mitchell repeatedly with a butcher's knife.

Eryn helps Evelyn off the floor, and they flee from the house.

The Selection Process

Jordan And The Black Falcons

30 years later...

Jordan sits in an alley in his car as he observes the gang members. The Black Falcons are a new gang, getting their start just five years ago. Like most gangs, they formed on good pretenses. To enforce positivity, good will, and protection among their community, which was infested with crime. But, like most gangs, they were soon overcome with greed, authority and power. Their good deeds shortly turned into evil deeds. Anything from prostitution to murder. Residents of the community used to turn to them for protection...now, they run from them, fearing for their lives.

"What's the word, Boss?" Jordan answers his phone.

"You got your eyes on them?"

"Yea. Got them locked in."

"The building set?"

"Yes. Just waiting for the clear."

"Good. Let me know when the deed is done." Click.

Jordan sits his phone down and continues to observe the gang from his car.

Earlier that day...

Jordan sits across from the alley as he observes the Black Falcons gang torturing another unfortunate victim.

"Please! Forgive me!"

"No second chances." The gang member threatens him. They start a blow torch and holds it up to his face. The man cries out in agony as the fire begins to scorch his face.

Present Day...

The members of the Black Falcons gang enters the old, decrepit house that has been boarded up for months.

Jordan presses a button on a remote. The house blows in an explosion. Jordan picks up his phone and dials a number.

"It's done." Click.

Jordan starts his car and drives from the dark alley. He pulls into the driveway of his house. He puts his car in park and kills the engine. He gets out of the car and enters his house.

Jordan gasps and struggles as he is attacked in the darkness of his living room. His body drops to the floor as he begins to lose consciousness.

Charlotte And The Special Collections

Charlotte moves quietly through the dark halls of the Kaleidoscope Library, being careful not to set off alarms that would alert the security guard. She enters the Special Collections Archives. She walks up to the item of interest: the original, unedited copy of *How To Unlock The Key To The Universe.* An informational guidebook written by the legendary, late Professor Theresa Guild in the early 1900s.

The book is available for public domain, but only the revised copies. Rumors have it that the original book contains sensitive material that is not to be accessed by unauthorized personnel, so it remains behind glass to be showcased.

Charlotte grabs her electric glass remover and places it on the glass. She makes a hole big enough to remove the book. An alarm sets off when she reaches her hand inside. She quickly grabs the book and flees the scene.

Charlotte manages to make it outside of the library before the security guard could catch her. She drops to the ground in shock as a taser clenches her back, sending a bolt of electricity through her body.

Dawn Has Skeletons In The Closet

Dawn stares at the grave of one of his victims. Five months ago, he lost his love to the ruthless attack of a group of heathens. One-by-one, he's made them pay the price of their consequences.

Dawn takes his shovel and begins to dig. He opens the casket and grabs the lifeless body of his once-victim to a vengeful murder. He puts the body in a trash bag and hauls the body over his shoulder and returns to his pick-up truck. He throws the body in the back of the truck and he gets in the car and drives off.

Dawn pulls into the driveway of his home. He puts the truck in park and turns off the ignition. He gets out and walks to the back of the truck to grab the body. He quickly enters his home.

Dawn drops the body on the floor to begin his work. His body freezes in place as he is injected with a syringe.

Victor And The Fraternity

Pastor Bron and his board of Deacons sit in the office as they conduct the next auction event. Once a month, they hold a live auction, where they sell a member of the clergy to the highest bidder. This helps to pay the bills of the church, as well as, keep the supply-and-demand flowing in other illegalities that they partake in.

The next woman is escorted in the office. Pastor Bron takes his video camera and targets the woman as she is forced to strip off all her clothes and showcase her nude body. He grins as the numbers begin to increase but expresses shock as a visitor makes an odd request.

Pastor Bron hands the camera to one of his Deacons. He unzips his pants and motions for the woman to suck his penis.

The woman drops down to her knees and crawls toward the Pastor. She edges closer, but Pastor Bron flinches at the sting of the syringe jabbed into his leg. He looks down at the woman, who grins sinisterly as his body drops to the floor.

Kane And The Mission Compromised

Kane, disguising himself as a Deacon, observes in shock as he witnesses the Pastor's body collapsing to the ground. That was supposed to be his job. He was on an assigned mission to terminate this church due to their unorthodox and inhumane activity.

Kane stands up from the crowd and displays his pocket blades. He begins to fight and slash his way through the Deacons. Realizing the Pastor and the woman has vanished from sight, he quickly flees the church after them.

Kane runs out into the cool night air. No one is in sight. He expresses shock as a car's engine roars and quickly makes its way towards him. He dodges the car. He takes his blade and flings it at the car, piercing one of the tires. He takes another blade and disables another tire.

The car begins to jerk from the impact of the tires being slashed. It eventually runs off the road, crashing into a tree.

Kane walks toward the car. He searches it for the Pastor's body but drops to the ground at the sting of the syringe piercing his neck.

Donald's Justice Is Served

Donald creeps in through the window of the house of the savage who took his family from him just two years prior. Since this fatal event, he has been on a never-ending journey to find their predator and make him pay. Along the way, he has taken the lives of other hard criminals, spreading vengeance and justice for the poor souls who have been victimized. Taking utmost care in this new role, Donald has disappeared from civilization and conformed to this lifestyle, taking the shine from the police force.

Donald slowly paces toward the noises coming from the living room. He peaks in the room. He observes as the three men play cards, smoke weed, and drink liquor. He displays his gun. He quickly dashes from the corner and shoots at the men.

The men scatter to flee the bullets but are quickly impacted. The target of Donald's target of interest crawls from the scene. Donald quickly walks toward him. He pulls a blade from his pocket. He grabs the man's head and runs the blade across his throat.

Donald drops to the floor as his shoulder is pierced by a syringe.

Peter's Next Stop...Nowhere

Peter punches the screaming woman, knocking her unconscious. He grabs her body, hauls it over his shoulder, and walks to his van. He opens the back of the van and hauls the woman inside with the other captives. He gets in the driver's seat and starts the engine. He drives off, merging in with traffic. Paul turns up the radio and he cruises along the highway.

♌

The driver kicks his engine into gear and charges at the van, running it off the road. He gets out the car and paces toward the van. He takes a syringe and jabs it into Peter's neck. He takes rope and ties his hands and feet. He grabs his unconscious body and returns to his car, hauling his body in the trunk of his car. The driver gets in the driver's seat and drives off.

Darryl And The Abduction Failure

D arryl quietly tampers with the lock of the door. It successfully unlocks, and he creeps into the house, closing the door behind him. He tiptoes up the staircase. He enters the nursery room of the baby he'd been eyeing since the neighbors returned home from the hospital. He creeps up to the baby's crib, and he gently picks up the sleeping baby. Cuddling it, he quietly leaves the house.

Opening the door to his car, Darryl lays the baby in the back seat. He gets in the driver's seat, starts the engine, and drives off.

The man quietly sits up from the floor of the car as Darryl drives. He displays a syringe, jabbing it in Darryl's neck.

Darryl's body goes into shock at the sting of the syringe. He loses control of the car as his body begins to lose consciousness.

Let The Games Begin

ScavengeReaper Introduced

Charlotte slowly regains consciousness. She observes her surroundings. The room is pitch black. She attempts to stand, but she is restrained.

"Hello?" She calls out. "Hello!"

A blinding light snaps on, radiating the room. Jordan, Peter, Pastor Bron, Darryl, Dawn, Kane, and Donald all regain consciousness as the light obstructs their vision. They observe their surroundings. All of them are restrained against the wall with contractions binding their hands and feet.

"What the hell is going on here?" Dawn shouts.

"Where are we?" Peter adds.

Everyone begins to argue and yell over each other. They fall silent when a television screen flickers on. Two unidentified people in masks display on the screen.

"Good evening all." A woman's voice beams through the hidden surround stereos, filling the room with an echo.

"Who are you?" Pastor Bron asks. "Why are we here?"

"Relax. You will find out what you need to know soon enough."

"We brought you here..." A man's voice starts. "Because you are the chosen ones."

"The chosen ones?" Darryl repeats. "What the hell does that mean?"

"We are going to play a game. It's called *ScavengeReaper*."

"Look, dude, I stopped playing games years ago." Kane says. "I ain't interested."

"If you had a choice, you wouldn't have been forced here. We chose you because this game requires certain people and special instructions. You are the only ones who can fill these roles."

"Excuse me?" Peter says. "What roles? What instructions?"

"You will get your instructions in a moment."

"First…" The woman says. "Let's introduce ourselves and get acquainted. Each of you must state your names and confess why you have been chosen. It does no good to pretend not to know. Each of you have an impact on society. Wrong or fake answers will reap consequences."

"What is this…school?" Kane says sarcastically.

"Furthermore, anyone talking out of turn will also reap consequences."

"Yes, mommy." Kane says sarcastically. "May I please go to the bathroom now? Fuck you, lady." Kane screams as his body is jolted with a shock.

"Care to continue?" The woman asks him. "We can keep this up. We have time." Kane falls silent.

"We will start with you, Charlotte Hortense."

Charlotte snaps her attention to the screen when she hears her name. "How do you know me?" She asks.

"That's not the activity." The woman says, losing patience. "State your name and why you are here."

"Bitch, you already know my name. And, evidently, I don't know why I'm here. How about you enlighten me." Charlotte screams as she feels the painful vibration spread through her body.

"My name is Charlotte Hortense and I am a college professor."

"What is your special hobby?"

"Special hobby?"

"Two nights ago, you were at the library. What were you doing there?"

"How do you know about that? Wait...you were the one who tased me that night."

"Congratulations. Now you know how you got here. What were you doing that led to your capture?"

"I was retrieving a book."

"Retrieving?"

"Okay, I was...stealing. Happy?"

"You are a thief. Is that something to be proud of?" Charlotte falls silent in her shame. "Next person. Now that we finally got Charlotte to answer the question right, this should be easy for the rest of you."

"My name is Peter Crane. I am a sales agent and a...trafficker."

"What do you traffic, Peter?"

"Women."

"I'm Victor Bron. I am a Pastor of Holy Temple. I...I'm not very different from Mr. Crane, here."

"Elaborate, Victor."

"My Deacons and I run a social club, called the Fraternity."

"What do you do in this social club?"

"We...auction off members of our clergy to a secret group of bidders on the dark web."

"I'm Kane Borris. I'm a paid hitman. I was *actually* on assignment to terminate Pastor Bron and The Fraternity...until *someone* got in my way and compromised my entire mission. Which *you two* can go to hell for." He says to the screen.

"Name's Jordan Carver. Kind of in the same line of work as Kane. But I target bad groups of people. People who do bad in society."

"People like you?" Jordan eyes the woman sinisterly.

"You're not in any predicament to judge me." Jordan snaps. "What about you and homeboy? You think this shit you're doing is good? Abducting and torturing people? You're no better than me."

"Never said we were. We know who we are. Unlike you, we don't go around facading."

"What does that even mean?"

"It means we all have a purpose in this world. My brother and I chose you based on your strengths and purposes. We're not here to judge you. We're here to welcome you."

"Please tell us how being abducted and held hostage in a basement is welcoming." Donald says. "Did I miss something, here?"

"Donald Travis. We almost forgot about you." The woman says. "Please introduce yourself."

"How about you do that? Seems like you already know who I am."

"Donald here suffered the pain of having his family taken from him. Although, unlike most normal citizens, he chose a different way to grieve. Didn't you, Donald?"

"That's right. You got me all figured out. I made that bastard pay for what he did to my family."

"But he's not the only one who paid. Is he?" Donald falls silent. "What about all of the innocent lives you took during your quest of vengeance?"

"Okay, we got it." Dawn interrupts. "We're all fucked up. So, tell us...what is this about? You're going to punish us?"

"Speaking of vengeance...Dawn Kurst. Please entertain us with your little side hobby. After you leave the office and get out of your fancy suits."

"I dig up graves."

"Why do you dig up graves?"

"I take bodies."

"And what do you do with these bodies? Don't hold out. Either you expose yourself or *we* do."

"I dig up graves, steal the corpses, and I hide them in my house."

"That's not all."

"I...I have sex with them."

"Ah yes...the necrophile. Actually, Dawn, *you* are our favorite. We love dead people too." The woman grins.

"I guess that leaves me. Not gonna let you two make a mockery of me." Darryl says. "Name's Darryl Wilson. I'm a Doctor."

"Oh, Darryl. And here, we thought you'd learned from your acquaintances. Doctor is only half of his job. Please tell us...what kind of Doctor are you?"

"I'm a Pediatrician."

"And, what does your "job" entail when you're not in the office? Your afterhours job."

"I abduct babies."

"And, what do you do with the babies?"

"I sell them on the Black Market in exchange for money."

"Now that we've all been acquainted; we can move on." The woman says.

"Evelyn and I are very much like you." The man says. "We, too, have an imprint to make on the world. You choose violence and corruption...we choose a more ritualistic way of doing things."

"Ritualistic?" Pastor Bron says. "What are you talking about?"

"Thirty years ago, our parents were sacrificed to a demon. I believe the event made headline news. You may or may not have heard about it."

"Yes, I remember the story. Don and Valerie Bobbins. They were Evangelists."

"Very good, Victor. Shortly after our parents passed away, we were put in the care of our Uncle Mitchell. The very guy who sacrificed them to a cult of Satanists. This cult attempted to revive the demon Zettagoryan."

"Zetta...who?" Charlotte asks out of confusion.

"Zettagoryan is a demon who takes evil souls. The legend goes that every 30 years on All Souls Day, Zettagoryan can be free of his prison to reign on Earth. He frees the world of evil souls. But...his resurrection requires a certain process. Only a human can free him. This is where you all come in." The man holds a book up to the screen.

SCAVENGEREAPER

"Scavengereaper?" Dawn reads. "What the hell does that mean?"

"ScavengeReaper is a game. The very game that holds the key to Zettagoryan's resurrection. We have already started the game...but we can't continue until we acquire the other components. *You.*"

"Us?" Kane says. "What does this have to do with *us*?"

"You all acquire the special skills that we need to complete this game and revive Zettagoryan...

Charlotte Hortense, the Bandit. Peter Crane, the Conductor. Kane Borris, the Assassin. Dawn Kurst, the Collector. Jordan Carver, the

Exterminator. Victor Bron, the Extortionist. Donald Travis, the Executioner. Darryl Wilson, the Abductor."

"How exactly do we fit into this game?" Peter asks.

"Look in your pockets. You each are given a character with special instructions. It is imperative you follow instructions and the time limit. All Souls Day is approaching. You have 48 hours to complete your tasks."

"Oh…and don't bother trying any funny business. We have tracking devices implanted in your flesh. We always know where you are. One more thing…we have tabs on a person closest to each of you. You fail to deliver…your loved ones pay the price."

"Complete the tasks by the time limit and meet back here no later than 11:00 p.m. on Halloween, and we let your loved ones go."

The group sighs in relief as their restraints are unlocked. They each search their pockets and locate their character cards.

"Time is ticking." The woman says. "No time to waste. Let the game begin."

Let The Games Begin

Charlotte And the Hidden Scroll

.

.

Charlotte reads over her character card again.

THE BANDIT

GO TO THE SENATOR'S HOUSE. IN THE SHED IN THE BACK YARD, THERE IS A SPECIAL DOCUMENT THAT IS SAFELY HIDDEN. RETRIEVE THE DOCUMENT AND RETURN WITH IT.

Charlotte tosses the card on her dresser and relaxes in her bed. She ponders how she's going to sneak her way on the Senator's territory without being shot dead before she could step on the lawn. Buildings, such as libraries and schools are easy tasks. Important people like the Senator weren't so easy. The police patrol the neighborhood like clockwork, taking extra precautions in the Senator's home.

On the same token...*what kind of document could the Senator have that these two psychos want? And what does the document have to do with the game?* Charlotte closes her eyes and drifts off to sleep.

⚲

The next morning, Charlotte jerks from her sleep, knowing how she will obtain the document. She figures since the Senator is usually busy early in the day, she will do it in the daytime.

Charlotte jumps from her bed. She quickly changes her clothes and throws on a pair of dingy jeans and a raggedy t-shirt. She brushes her hair up into a messy bun and ties a scarf around it. She leaves out the house and gets into her car.

Charlotte drives up to the corner of the Senator's street. She observes the police car that sits parked across the from house. She grabs a pair of gloves and a trash bag from the back seat and hesitantly steps out of the car.

Charlotte strolls up the street to the yard of the Senator's house and starts observing the weeds. She jumps when she feels a tap on her shoulder.

"Jesus, you scared me!" She snaps at the police officer.

"Ma'am, can I help you?" The officer asks her. "What is your business on this property? And why do you have a trash bag and gloves?"

"Oh...I'm Natasha. I'm the gardener."

"The gardener? I don't believe I've seen you around here before."

"Oh, I work part time. I usually only come on Sundays but had some free time today and thought I'd stop by and check out the yard. Make sure hedges don't need trimming and whatnot."

"Okay, Ma'am. Make it quick."

"Don't need long at all." Charlotte exhales when the officer returns to his car. She begins to pick the weeds in the front yard. She breathes a sigh of relief when she notices him drive away. She slips to the back yard to the shed. To no surprise, it's locked.

"Shit!" She curses to herself. She observes the yard for something to use to open the lock. She locates a brick in the garden. She runs over to the garden to take a brick and returns to the shed. She instantly begins hitting the lock until it breaks open. She rips it off the door and disappears into the shed, closing the door behind her.

Charlotte clicks on the handy lamp on the side table. She scours the place. "No wonder she has this place bolted up." Charlotte thinks out loud. "Senator's into some twisted shit." Charlotte frowns as she observes the collection of creepy voodoo dolls and crosses that decorate the place. She looks through a pile of magic books that sits in the corner.

She then notices a weird picture that is taped to the wall with a newspaper clipping. She gets closer to read the article.

"A CULT OF SATANISTS

ACCUSED OF SACRIFICING

A COUPLE OF EVANGELISTS"

Charlotte expresses a look of shock as she recalls the mention of events from Evelyn and Eryn. "Oh shit!" Charlotte gasps. "Let me hurry and find this damn document before Senator sacrifices my ass too."

Charlotte quickly scours the shed. She stops when her foot catches on something. She investigates and notices a loose floorboard. She opens it and looks inside. She discovers a box. She reaches in and grabs it. She opens the box and looks inside.

She notices an old scroll. "This must be what they want." She thought to herself. She opens the scroll and reads.

يا مظلم واحد ...

نحن ندعوك الان

صعود من العالم السفلي.

خذ مكانك بين الأحياء.

يا مظلم واحد ...

نحن ندعوك الان

صعود من العالم السفلي.

خذ مكانك بين الأحياء.

"What the hell kind of shit is this?" Charlotte says, reading the scroll. "Looks like Arabic language. Wonder if it's a voodoo spell."

Charlotte expresses a look of terror when she hears a car in the driveway. "Shit! Senator must be back home." She slips the scroll in her back pocket, kills the light from the lamp and finds a corner to hide in.

ະ

Ten hours later...

Charlotte observes through the crack of the shed's door, as she waits patiently for the Senator to retire for the night. She exhales when she sees the lights in the house turn off. She inhales and exhales again before she quietly opens the shed's door and makes a run for it.

Charlotte freezes in her tracks when she notices the police officer has returned to his spot across the street from the Senator's house.

"Fuck!" She whispers to herself. "Think, Charlotte. Think."

Charlotte runs behind the shed, and she begins to climb the fence. She expresses a look of horror when the Rottweilers from the next yard begin to bark at her and struggle against their chains. She lands on the pavement of the neighbor's yard, just missing the dogs' perimeter. She scrambles to stand up from the ground and flee the yard, jumping over the next fence. She continues this until she's at a safe enough distance from the police officer.

Charlotte paces out of the neighbor's yard and innocently walks back to her car. She jumps in, starts the engine, and drives off.

Victor And The Temple Of Gulles

V ictor reads his card.

THE EXTORTIONIST

VISIT THE TEMPLE OF GULLES. ABDUCT THE PRIEST. DELIVER HIM ALIVE.

Victor lays down on his bed and rests his eyes. He awakes the next morning and takes his shower. He eats his routine breakfast of bacon, eggs and toast with a cup of coffee. He leaves the house and gets in his car.

Victor pulls into the parking lot of the Temple of Gulles. Everyone knows of the evil things these people do, but they've only heard through gossip and rumors. If you weren't a member of the Temple, then you didn't know what went on behind closed doors.

Gaining membership isn't easy. There are some steps to take for initiation. Similar to hazing for a sorority or a fraternity.

Victor rings the buzzer on the side of the door.

"Catchphrase." A voice beams on the intercom.

"Actually...I'm here to join." Victor responds into the intercom. Brief silence.

"State your name."

"Frank Morton." A loud buzz sounds. Victor pulls at the door and walks inside.

"Follow me." The guard that stands at the door says. He leads Victor to an office. "Have a seat. Father Hector will be with you shortly."

Victor sits in the seat across from the Priest's desk. He observes the pictures that decorate the office's walls.

"Mr. Morton." Father Hector greets him as he enters the office.

Victor stands to shake his hand. "Father."

"Please...call me Hector for now. Save the legalities for later." Victor sits back down as Father Hector takes his seat behind the desk. "Officer Jacks tells me you're interested in joining us."

"Yes, sir."

"If I may...what is your religion?"

"I was born and raised Christian."

"Are you aware of what we are?"

"Yes I am. I've done my research."

"So, tell me...why are you interested in converting over?"

"My religion has failed me many times. I thought I knew it all, but I don't. Looking for a new meaning to life."

"You know, there are many other religions and churches out there."

"Yes. None of them strike my attention more than this one."

"What is it about our practices that strike you?"

"Your morals. Your way of thinking."

"Of course, you know there's an initiation process that you first must pass before you gain membership to the Temple Of Gulles."

"I am aware."

"When would you like to start?"

"I am ready now."

"Today is your lucky day. I happen to be free all day. I will make the preparations." Father Hector speaks into the intercom. "Officer Jacks, will you please come to the office?"

The guard enters the door. "Jacks, please help Mr. Morton get ready for his initiation. And prepare the sanctuary and gather the others."

"Yes, Father."

"You're in good hands, Mr. Morton." Father Hector says. "Jacks will take it from here. I will prepare and I will see you momentarily."

Victor stands up from the chair and follows the guard's lead. They walk into a room that's designed like a bedroom.

"You will find a robe in the chest." The guard says. "Undress completely and put on the robe. I will be right outside the door. Press the intercom to alert me when you are ready." The guard leaves the room, closing the door behind him.

Victor immediately begins to undress. He folds his street clothes neatly on the bed and drapes the robe over his nude body. He presses the intercom to alert the guard.

The guard opens the door and motions for Victor to follow him. They enter a dining room. Father Hector sits at one end of the table. A group of men sit in the middle chairs. The guard motions Victor to sit at the opposite end.

"Mr. Morton, meet the clan." Father Hector says. "You will get more acquainted with them after you successfully past initiation."

Victor focuses his attention as the Cook enters the dining room with a plate. She sits the plate in front of Victor. He gags as he sees the freshly killed, uncooked rat.

"Your first test is to eat what is on your plate." Father Hector says to Victor. "We at the Temple of Gulles have a very...natural diet."

Victor grows nauseous as he eyes the dead rodent. He picks up the fork and knife and begins to eat, struggling to devour it and refrain from getting sick. He gulps down the glass of water.

The guard motions Victor to following him into the next room. A young, nude woman rests on the bed with her hands chained to the headboard. "Don't worry." Father Hector says. "She's not dead. Just heavily sedated. Your next test is to have sex with a virgin."

"If I may...how old is she?"

"Twelve."

Victor grows more nauseous at the thought of raping a drugged-up underage girl. He's done some questionable things in his life, but he'd never do something as bad as this. Then Victor remembers the main reason he's here, and he thinks of his daughter, Melody. If he doesn't follow through, she pays the price.

Victor disrobes and approaches the unconscious woman. He strokes his penis until he gets an erection. He holds the girl's limp body while he thrusts inside of her. He grunts as he ejaculates.

Victor clenches his eyes as he is overcome with shame. He pulls out of the girl and scrambles to drape the robe over his body.

Victor follows Father Hector and the guard to another room. "Your final test." Father Hector says. "You must be cleansed of your old religion and baptized into your new religion."

Victor stares, speechless, at the bathtub that's filled with blood. *Who's blood is this?* Victor thinks to himself. He grows lightheaded as he feels his stomach churn from the unsavory dinner he'd had.

Victor forces himself to focus on the mission. He disrobes and eases his body into the blood-filled bathtub. Hector approaches the side of the tub. He kneels down and grasps Victor's head in his hands. He submerges Victor's head under the blood.

Victor struggles to hold his breath as he is forced under the blood. A moment later, Hector releases his hold on Victor's head. Victor jerks from the blood, choking on the blood that has made its way into his mouth.

"Welcome, Brother Morton." Father Hector says as he plants a kiss on Victor's forehead. "You have successfully passed initiation."

⚓

Victor sits in his bedroom, in his clean suit that has been provided for him. Privileges for those who pass initiation and baptize themselves into the Temple of Gulles. Officer Jacks knocks on the door and enters. He motions Victor to follow him. They walk into a conference room. There sits Father Hector and the other men that were present at the dining table during Victor's first step of initiation.

"Brother Frank." Father Hector said. "Its time for you to meet the clan. These are deacons but we are all family here, so we call refer to each other as Brothers. You can make your rounds and personally introduce yourselves later. Everyone here addresses me as Father."

"Nice to meet you, Brothers."

Father Hector stands and motions Victor to follow him into the next room. "Here, we have our deaconess committee. We refer to them as our Sisters. Ladies, this is our new addition, Brother Victor Morton."

Father Hector continues to the next room. "This is our cooks, servants, and hostesses. Ladies, meet our new addition, Brother Victor Morton."

Father Hector continues on down a staircase. "These rooms belong to our children. Right side is the girls, left side is the boys. We refer to them as Sons and Daughters."

"During your membership to the Temple Of Gulles, it is imperative that you live on the premises. We like to stay together as a family at all times. I can help you make moving arrangements if you'd like."

"No, thank you, Father." Victor says. "I will call a moving company. I should be all settled in by tomorrow afternoon."

"Great. Welcome again."

☙

Victor returns to his house to prepare a small overnight bag. He figures if he's going to abduct Father Hector, the only sure way would be to get in his good graces first. He leaves the house with his overnight bag and returns to the Temple.

The sun is beginning to set. Victor glances at his watch. He has approximately 36 hours to complete his mission.

☙

7 hours later...

Victor rests against his bed as he waits for the crew to retire for the night. He snaps into focus when he hears a knock on his bedroom door. He expresses surprise when Father Hector enters his room, closing and locking the door behind him.

"Good evening, Brother Frank." Father Hector greets him.

"Good evening, Father. Is everything okay?"

"Just making my nightly rounds to check up on everyone and make sure everything is okay. Thought I'd start with you since you are our newest addition. How is the room?"

"It's good. I called the moving company. The earliest they are available is tomorrow afternoon. I just grabbed me a small overnight bag for tonight."

"Good. Good. I did forget to mention one tiny detail as part of joining the Temple."

"What's that?" Father Hector disrobes, displaying his nude body before Victor.

Victor grows light-headed at the sight of Father Hector's erection. He cringes at the gesture. "Well...I let me go and freshen up quickly. I've been lazy since I've been back."

Victor disappears into the bathroom, closing the door behind him. He runs the water. He quickly scours his utility bag for the syringe he'd acquired prior to returning to the Temple. He slides it in his back pocket. He takes off his shirt and splashes water on his face and brushes his teeth. He turns off the water and opens the bathroom door.

Victor returns to the bedroom, where Father Hector has made himself comfortable. "So...what exactly am I supposed to do?" He asks him.

Father Hector stands up from the bed and leans up against the wall. "On your knees." He says to Victor.

Victor walks up before Father Hector and kneels down before him. He hesitantly eases his erect penis in his mouth. Father Hector grunts and moans as Victor sucks him off.

Victor reaches for the syringe from his back pocket. He jabs it into Father Hector's leg. Father Hector's moans turns into faint grunts as his body begins to process the substance. He drops to the floor as he slowly loses consciousness.

Victor walks to the bedroom door and peeks outside. He scours the halls. No one is in sight. He quietly paces toward the back entrance to the Temple. Officer Jacks sits by the door and rests his head against the wall.

Victor returns to the bedroom. He looks out the window. He opens the latch and pushes the window up. Exhales a sigh of relief. He grabs

Father's Hector's body and lunges him out the window. Fortunately for him, they are only two stories high, so the impact won't be bad. Victor grabs his overnight bag and escapes out the window.

He drags Father Hector's unconscious body to his car. He opens the trunk and hauls him inside, closing the trunk's door. He gets in the car, starts the engine, and drives off.

Darryl And The Little Eagles Sanctuary

D arryl reads his card.

THE ABDUCTOR

VISIT <u>THE LITTLE EAGLES SANCTUARY</u>. FIND THE FOLLOWING KIDS: BRITTANY BRANCH, JOSEPHINE KNIGHT, SARA STEVENS, JOSHUA ADAMS, CHARLIE TURK. DELIVER THEM ALIVE.

Darryl rests against his bed as he thinks about how he's going to abduct a bunch of kids. You'd think this would be right up his alley since he's been abducting kids and selling them to the black market for five years now.

"What's so special about these kids, anyway?" Darryl begins to ponder. "What do they want with them?"

Darryl grabs his Mac Book Pro and begins to search the internet. He types in the address for the Little Eagles Sanctuary.

Welcome to The Little Eagles Sanctuary.

This is a place where your kids can grow and enhance their skills to a new level. A new way of thinking. A new way of life. The Eagles Way.

The Little Eagles Sanctuary formed in the 1900s by original board members Oscar Branch, Doris Knight, Gregory Stevens, Janay Adams, Carlisle Turk, and Heather Givens.

Darryl looks at the card and reads the names of the kids again. He pulls up another browser and begins to search up the names of the board members separately.

Oscar Branch, City Council, Ward 1, deceased.

Doris Knight, City Council, Ward 2, deceased.

Gregory Stevens, City Council, Ward 3, deceased.

Janay Adams, City Council, Ward 4, deceased.

Carlisle Turk, City Council, Ward 5, deceased.

Heather Givens, City Council, Ward 6, deceased.

"These all used to be members of the city council." Darryl thought as he calculated the analysis. "So, that means, these kids must be their great-great-great-great grandkids. This still doesn't make sense."

Darryl accesses GoogleScholar to research further. He scrolls down and clicks on an article.

"A CULT OF SATANISTS

ACCUSED OF SACRIFICING

A COUPLE OF EVANGELISTS"

Darryl pauses as he recalls the conversation with Evelyn and Eryn. "They must be the cult that sacrificed their parents. But...what could they want with the kids?" His eyes getting heavy, Darryl puts his computer to the side and goes to sleep.

♋

The next morning, Darryl prepares for his venture to the Little Eagles Sanctuary. He grabs his suitcase and leaves the house. He drives in the parking lot of the Little Eagles Sanctuary. He grabs his suitcase and walks to the door. He rings the buzzard. An alarm sounds and he enters the door.

"Can I help you?" A security guard asks him.

"Yes…I'm Mr. Stone. I applied for employment and have an interview this morning."

"Ah, yes. Welcome, Mr. Stone. My name is Ms. Freeling. I will be conducting your interview today. Mr. Moss has been expecting you. He's very pleased with your resume. We haven't had a candidate like you in years."

"I'm excited to be here. I love kids. Been working at the hospital for a while, but recently the staff has changed tremendously, underwent new management and things haven't been the same."

"I definitely understand that. While we have had different bosses, we are fortunate that all of them have stuck to our traditions. The children here are all great kids. We teach them strong ethics and morals that we believe all kids should learn. It sets them up for great futures."

"Yes, I've researched as much as I could before applying. Its one of the reasons I was motivated to apply. Kids need a strong foundation and I believe you guys provide that."

"We do the best to our ability. Some teachings the kids don't agree with, but they will understand soon enough."

"Like what, if I may ask?"

"For instance...this whole addiction to technology. We believe there is more to life than technology. So...we've enforced a strict 1 hour-a-day television policy. The rest of the day is to be used toward meaningful connections and engaging activities, such as reading, school, extracurricular activities."

"Sounds reasonable to me. I definitely agree with that philosophy."

"We are glad you do. Previous staff members didn't agree too much. Tried to bend the guidelines and make new policies. So, we had to get rid of them."

"I don't blame you. That's what happened when the hospital went under new management. Everything changed almost overnight. No advanced warning to get acquainted with the new way of things. So, everything we've been trained to do before was suddenly the wrong way."

"We believe in the old school way of life. The way our ancestors were taught and instilled in us."

"I couldn't agree more."

"Well...Mr. Stone. I have given you a rundown of our guidelines. You have certainly passed my test. When can you start?"

"Is today available?"

"Today is perfect. Consider this your crash course. I will start you off with Mrs. Grimes. She will take you on a whole tour of the facility and get you acquainted with the different classrooms. Mr. Moss is currently out of the office, but he should be back tomorrow. You will meet him then."

"Great. Thank you so much."

"Pleasure to have you." Ms. Freeling says, shaking his hand. "Mr. Grimes will take it from here." Ms. Freeling walks away.

"Welcome, Mr. Stone. I am Mrs. Freeling. I am the caretaker here at The Little Eagles Sanctuary."

"Pleasure to meet you." Darryl shakes her hand.

※

After his tour of The Little Eagles Sanctuary, Darryl leaves and returns home to get some rest. He has an eventful day tomorrow.

.ł.

The next morning, Darryl eats his breakfast and takes his shower. He puts on a nice suit for his first official day of work at The Little Eagles Sanctuary. He grabs his suitcase and leaves the house.

He returns to The Little Eagles Sanctuary and parks his car in the reserved section for employees. He grabs his suitcase and gets out the car. He walks to the employee entrance and swipes his badge at the intercom. The alarm sounds. He walks inside.

"Good morning, Mr. Stone." Ms. Freeling greets him. "Are you ready for your first day?"

"Yes I am."

"Mrs. Grimes showed you your office?"

"Yes, ma'am."

"Great, well you go ahead and get settled in. Mr. Moss is in his office and is expecting you shortly."

"Thank you." Darryl continues to his office. He sits his suitcase next to his desk and leaves back out.

Darryl knocks on the door of Mr. Moss' office. "Come in." He opens the door. "Mr. Moss. Ms. Freeling has told me all great things about you. It is a pleasure to have you on board."

"The pleasure is all mine, sir. Thank you for this opportunity."

"And I know Mrs. Grimes was able to give you the crash course here. Today, don't worry about the heavy lifting. Continue getting acquainted with the building and the kids. I'm sure they'll be pleased to meet you."

"Thank you so much, sir." Darryl leaves the office, closing the door behind him.

He returns to his office and turns on the computer. He pulls up his email and browses through the new messages. He clicks on the message titled: **Staff And Student Directory**. He grabs a notepad and browses the list, making a note of the names of his interest and their classroom numbers.

Darryl leaves his office and paces down the hallways, checking in on the different classrooms the kids of his mission are in. He pops in to engage with them enough to make them comfortable.

Returning to his office, Darryl picks up his office phone and dials a number. "Hello, Ms. Freeling. This is Stone. I just came back from making my rounds and getting acquainted with the teachers and kids. I was wondering…would it be out of line if I took a few of the kids on a brief field trip today? Just a few that have opened up to me a little more than the others. Just want to take them to the Natural History Museum. Maybe that's why we connected so well because I love dinosaurs as well."

"You must be speaking of Brittany Branch, Josephine Knight, Sara Stevens, Joshua Adams, and Charlie Turk."

"Yes, that's them."

"Those little sly devils got to you too, I see?" Chuckle. "Well, the only way that would be approved of is if Mrs. Grimes goes along. She's been the designated nurse before you came, and she knows all their illnesses and allergies. She will get you trained and caught up on it all."

"That is fine. Thank you."

"I will get the limo ready for you all."

Limo? These are certainly rich people. No wonder tuition costs so much. Darryl grabs his suitcase and waits by the entrance of the school for the kids. Luckily, he brought enough spare syringes. Just in case.

The driver pulls into the parking lot of the Natural History Museum. He gets out and opens the doors, helping the kids out of the limo. Darryl grabs his suitcase and gets out the limo.

They all walk into the Natural History Museum. Darryl shows the check-in person his employee badge. "How many?" The check-in person asks.

"Five children and two adults." She keys in the numbers on the register and presents seven admission wristbands.

"Have a great day." She says.

"Thank you." Darryl puts the wristbands on all of the wrists and they walk into the museum.

"Thank you so much, Mr. Stone!" Charlie says. "We've been wanting to come here for a while."

"You all go and play. Just remember, we have to be back by 1 p.m. You have two hours to play." The kids run off into the museum.

"This is so sweet of you, Mr. Stone." Mrs. Grimes says to him. "The kids don't get out often. Besides recess on the school grounds. I'm surprised Ms. Freeling trusted you enough to let you conduct this field trip. They are usually very strict."

"Well...they have a good set of morals. I can understand."

"I have to use the restroom." Mrs. Grimes says. "I will be right back." She walks off.

Darryl walks after her with his suitcase in hand. He takes out a syringe. He quietly opens the door to the women's restroom and sneaks into a stall. He peeks out the crack of the stall door. When Mrs. Grimes walks out of the stall, he quickly walks out, takes the syringe, and jabs it in her neck.

Mrs. Grimes' body drops to the floor and jerks as the poison spreads through her body. Darryl drags her into a stall and rests her on the toilet. He strolls out of the women's restroom and out to the parking lot.

Darryl approaches the limo. The driver is resting in the seat, his head leaned back on the headboard. Darryl takes out another syringe with poison and jabs it in his neck. The driver's body jerks around before letting the poison take him. He falls limp against the seat.

Darryl puts his suitcase in the limo. He opens the driver's car and drags his unconscious body out and puts him in the trunk.

Darryl walks inside of the museum to find the kids. "Hey, guys, its time to go now."

The kids all gathered in a line in front of Darryl. They file out of the museum and to the limo.

"Where's Mrs. Grimes and Mr. Stenz?" Josephine asks Darryl.

"They had an emergency to tend to back at the school. They left me in charge of getting you kids back." Darryl opens the limo door and they all file into the limo. "Here is some water for you all." He says, handing them the bottles of water laced with the substance from the syringes.

He gets in the driver's seat, starts the engine, and drives off.

Dawn And The Black Owles Cemetery

Dawn reads his card.

THE COLLECTOR

VISIT <u>THE BLACK OWLES CEMETERY</u>. DIG UP
THE BODIES OF THE FOLLOWING PEOPLE:
OSCAR BRANCH, DORIS KNIGHT, GREGORY
STEVENS, JANAY ADAMS, CARLISLE TURK,
AND HEATHER GIVENS. DELIVER THE BODIES
HERE.

Dawn tosses the card to the side and rests on his bed as he thinks about how he's going to transport these bodies back to the warehouse. He's used to digging up one or two bodies at a time. Not several. It takes him 20-30 minutes to dig up one body. 6 bodies is going to take him hours. Plus, his car is a 1997 Honda Civic. No way that many bodies are going to fit in there.

I wonder what's so special about these bodies, anyway. Dawn thought to himself. He grabs his laptop and begins to do some research on the names.

Oscar Branch (1929 -1989), City Council, Ward 1. Deceased. Death by fire.

Doris Knight (1929 – 1989), City Council, Ward 2. Deceased. Death by fire.

Gregory Stevens (1929 – 1989), City Council, Ward 3. Deceased. Death by fire.

Janay Adams (1929 – 1989), City Council, Ward 4. Deceased. Death by fire.

Carlisle Turk (1929 – 1989), City Council, Ward 5. Deceased. Death by fire.

Heather Givens (1929 – 1989), City Council, Ward 6. Deceased. Death by fire.

"They all died the same time and the same way. They were all the same age. They would have been in their 90s today. That's strange." Dawn researches further.

"A CULT OF SATANISTS

ACCUSED OF SACRIFICING

A COUPLE OF EVANGELISTS"

"CITY COUNCIL MEMBERS

BELIEVED TO BE ASSOCIATED

WITH A CULT"

"CITY COUNCIL MEMBERS

BELIEVED TO BE PRACTICING

SATANISM"

"CITY COUNCIL MEMBERS

FOUND DEAD.

CAUSE OF DEATH: MASS EXPLOSION"

"What the hell was city council into?" Dawn then recalls the conversation with Evelyn and Eryn.

"They must have been part of the cult that sacrificed their parents. But these guys have been dead for 30 years. Their bodies are probably rotted by now."

Dawn gags at the thought of a decomposed corpse in his car.

"Those assholes are going to owe me a new car after this."

Dawn turns off his laptop and puts it to the side. He turns off the bedroom light and goes to sleep.

♟

The next afternoon, Dawn prepares his car for the venture. He covers the interior with plastic to keep the rotting corpses from messing up his seats. He puts plastic in the trunk of the car. He figures he can at least fit one corpse in the trunk. Maybe two if he positions them right.

♟

Eight hours later...

Dawn parks his car around the corner from the Black Owles Cemetery as he waits for the caretaker to close for the day. Since this job is going to take him at least 3 hours, he wants to get an early start so he's not there all night.

Dawn observes as the caretaker locks the entrance gate, gets in his car, and drives off. He starts his car and creeps up to the gate. He gets out the car, walks up to the gate and searches for a hidden compartment. One thing he's learned in this hobby of his, is that all caretakers leave a spare key in case they lose the main key.

When Dawn locates the compartment, he reaches in and grabs the spare key. He quickly opens the gate to the cemetery, jumps in his car, and drives through the gate before anyone notices him. He stops a few feet from the gate, gets out, and locks it behind him. He gets back in the car and drives further into the cemetery.

Dawn quickly scours the cemetery, reading the headstones. When he locates his group, he is relieved to see they are all gathered in the same area. He returns to his car to grab his gloves and shovel, and he gets to work digging up the graves.

Dawn pauses for breath when he finishes digging up the last body. Exhausted, he sluggishly drags the corpse to his car and piles it on top of the others. He wastes no time in jumping in his car and fleeing the cemetery, relieved to not have gotten caught.

Kane And The Temple Of Crowes

Kane reads his card.

THE ASSASSIN

VISIT <u>THE TEMPLE OF CROWES</u>. MURDER THE MEMBERS. DELIVER THEIR BODIES HERE.

Kane grabs his laptop and searches up The Temple Of Crowes.

Welcome to The Temple Of Crowes.

This is a place where you can grow and enhance your mind to a new level. A new way of thinking. A new way of life. The Crowes Way.

The Temple Of Crowes formed in the 1900s by original board members Oscar Branch, Doris Knight, Gregory Stevens, Janay Adams, Carlisle Turk, and Heather Givens.

Kane researches more.

"TEMPLE OF CROWES UNDER INVESTIGATION"

"MEMBERS OF TEMPLE OF

CROWES BELIEVED TO

PRACTICE SATANISM"

"THE TEMPLE OF CROWES:

A CULT OF DEVIL WORHIPERS?"

Kane starts searching up the names of the board members.

Oscar Branch (1929 -1989), City Council, Ward 1. Deceased. Death by fire.

Doris Knight (1929 – 1989), City Council, Ward 2. Deceased. Death by fire.

Gregory Stevens (1929 – 1989), City Council, Ward 3. Deceased. Death by fire.

Janay Adams (1929 – 1989), City Council, Ward 4. Deceased. Death by fire.

Carlisle Turk (1929 – 1989), City Council, Ward 5. Deceased. Death by fire.

Heather Givens (1929 – 1989), City Council, Ward 6. Deceased. Death by fire.

Getting sleepy, Kane retires his search and falls asleep.

The next morning, Kane prepares for his venture to The Temple Of Crowes. During his search, he knows that the church is into some weird shit. During his career as a hitman, he is used to weird shit. Yet, he has never come across devil worshipers.

Kane packs his utility bag, consisting of a variety of his favorite weapons he uses to complete his missions. He takes his shower and puts on his favorite black suit, shirt, and tie. He slides on his black dress shoes.

He scarfs down his quick breakfast of eggs and toast. He grabs his utility bag and leaves the house.

Kane drives into the parking lot of The Temple Of Crowes. He rings the buzzer.

"Catchphrase." A voice beams into the intercom.

"I'm looking to gain membership to the temple." Kane responds. A brief pause. An alarm sounds. Kane opens the door and walks inside.

"Follow me." The guard orders Kane. He leads him into an office.

"Ah, come in." The man says. "Thank you, Bane." The guard leaves the office and closes the door.

"I hear you want to join The Temple of Crowes."

"Yes sir."

"I'm Father Graham. Luckily, we have an open spot. There a few steps you must take. First step is the application process." He presents a paper application.

Kane takes the paper and reads over it.

TEMPLE OF CROWES

MEMBERSHIP APPLICATION

NAME:

DATE OF BIRTH:

ADDRESS:

WHY DO YOU WANT TO JOIN THE TEMPLE OF CROWES?

WHAT ARE YOUR RELIGIOUS BELIEFS?

DESCRIBE A PIVOTAL POINT IN YOUR LIFE WHERE YOU HAD TO MAKE A TOUGH CHOICE.

Kane grabs a pen and begins to answer the questions. He hands the application to Father Graham, who browse over his answers.

"Interesting." Father Graham mumbles. "Well, Mr. Sharpe, based on your application, you will fit in well here. The next phase is initiation. You will have three tests. Upon successful completion of each test, you will move over to the final phase. Are you ready to begin?"

"Yes, sir."

Father Graham presses the button and speaks into the intercom. "Bane, come into the office, please." The guard opens the door. "Please get Mr. Sharpe ready for initiation."

"Yes, Father." The guard motions for Kane to follow him. He leads him to a dining room. The guard orders Kane to sit down.

Father Graham turns on the surveillance equipment in his office. He relaxes in his chair as he observes Kane.

Kane focuses his attention as the cook walks into the dining room and sits a plate on the table before him. She removes the cover, displaying a raw, uncooked, slab of meat. She sits a glass of red wine on the table next to the plate.

Kane grows lightheaded as he eyes the plate. He has been a vegetarian for ten years after witnessing the mutilation of a deer. He has been committed to the lifestyle ever since. Seeing the slab of raw meat brought back the horrible memories of the event that has left an imprint on him. Now, every time he sees meat, he is forced to think of that stomach-churning event.

Kane inhales. He holds his breath for a moment. Then he exhales. He picks up the knife and fork and begins to eat the meat. He starts to sweat as the meat makes its way down his throat. He clenches his eyes shut to force the meat to settle. When he finishes the last bite, he gulps down the wine.

The guard motions Kane to follow him into the next room. There lies an unconscious body. The head is covered with a sheet. The hands tied by ropes.

Kane's stomach begins to churn from his dinner and from the assumption at what this could mean. He has to have sex with a dead body. He grows nauseous as he looks at the legs that dangle halfway off the bed. He glances at the guard, who stands quietly in the corner of the room.

Kane begins to undress from the waist down. He strokes his penis to get an erection, but he finds it hard. He glances at the lotion and the magazine that sits on the dresser. He grabs the magazine and opens it, revealing the nude porn models. He instantly becomes erected.

Kane spreads the dead woman's legs and enters her. He looks at the porn magazine while he thrusts inside of her. He grunts when he ejaculates.

Kane quickly gets dressed and follows the guard to the next room. They enter a basement, where a live lamb is chained to the wall. Kane stumbles as his eyesight becomes blurry. The memories of the deer floods his mind. Kane focuses as the guard places an object in his hand. An axe.

Kane stumbles from blurred visions as he slowly approaches the helpless animal. He lifts the axe and begins to attack the lamb. A black veil drapes over Kane's face as the lamb cries out.

Kane stops his attacks on the lamb and snaps his attention to the guard that stands in the corner of the room. He charges at the guard and flings the axe in his direction. The guard drops to the floor, screaming as the axe clashes with his head. Kane grabs the axe from his head and finishes the job, chopping off his head.

Kane panics as he hears feet charging to the basement. He scrambles to find a corner to hide. He observes as the gang of men rush into the basement. Eight men. Not including Father Graham. That makes a total of nine men he must kill.

Kane takes a second to think about how he's going to kill them. He left his utility bag in the car. He remembers the syringes of poison he slipped into his pocket before leaving the car. He takes out the three syringes and flings them at three of the men. They drop to the floor from the impact of the poison.

Kane ducks for cover as the other men draw their guns and begins to open fire. He takes out a pocket blade and flings it at one of the men. He remains hidden until they run out of ammunition. Kane runs from his hiding spot and charges at the men. He grabs the axe from the guard's head and begins to slash his way through the gang.

Kane looks around the basement that is decorated with the bead bodies of the men. He then remembers Father Graham. He grabs the axe and makes his way back to the office.

Kane freezes as he is held at gunpoint by Father Graham.

"You thought you could outsmart me." Father Graham said. "You know...this city talks. I've heard of you. The hitman who's paid to murder members of churches. I was wondering when I'd get to finally meet the man behind the mask. Drop it." Kane drops the axe to the floor.

He reaches into his back pocket for his pocketknife. He flings the blade at Father Graham's wrist. Father Graham panics at the pain of the blade piercing his wrist. His finger pulls on the trigger and the gun goes off. Kane ducks for cover until the bullets stop. He grabs the axe and walks toward Father Graham, who rests on the floor, cradling his injured hand.

"You know...you won't get away with this forever." Father Graham says. "One day, you will meet your maker." Kane raises the axe and hauls it at his chest, piercing his flesh. Father Graham's body falls limp to the floor.

Kane goes to work at wrapping up the bodies and loading them in his truck.

Jordan And The Hawkes Mansion

J ordan reads his card.

THE EXTERMINATOR

**VISIT <u>THE HAWKES MANSION</u>. MURDER THE
MEMBERS OF THE HAWKES PARTY. DELIVER
THEIR BODIES HERE.**

Jordan has heard of The Hawkes Mansion and
The Hawkes Party on multiple occasions, but
only through reputation and rumors. He doesn't

know how true the allegations are, but he knows that they are a bad crowd. He's tried to do research on them, but the results don't bring up anything of interest. Just the basic knowledge of the party. You know as much as they want you to know. You must be an insider to gain inside information.

Jordan doesn't need to be an insider to know that this is a bad bunch of people. Their reputation precedes themselves. He's heard rumors from counts of drug activity to mass murders and anything in between.

Little do Evelyn and Erin know, the Hawkes Party has been on Jordan's hit list for a while now. Killing them is the easy part. Gaining access into the Mansion will be hard. Jordan has circled the place a few times during his commutes. They have the place guarded like a prison. Guards posted around the building. Guards patrolling the area like clockwork.

Jordan picks up his phone and dials a number.

"Aye, Boss. You wouldn't happen to have any insider information on The Hawkes Mansion, would you?"

"Nothing more of what you know, unfortunately. I've been trying to dig up information on it for years. They are very good at hiding."

"Tell me about it. There's close to nothing online."

"Nothing that we can see, at least. I've heard people say that you can find all kinds of information on them on the dark web. But you know I don't mess around with stuff like that."

"Right. I'm going to see what I can dig up. I will holla at you later." Click.

Jordan grabs his throwaway laptop and goes to the Tor Project website. He begins the download process.

After the software successfully installs and he has access, he begins his research on The Hawkes Party.

"HAWKES MANSION: THE SITE

OF HORRIFIC MURDERS"

"THE HAWKES PARTY BELIEVED

TO ENGAGE IN OCCULT

PRACTICES"

"THE HAWKES PARTY ACCUSED

OF SACRIFICING A COUPLE

OF EVANGELISTS"

Jordan recalls Evelyn and Eryn mentioning their parents being sacrificed by a cult of Satanists. He keeps scrolling, and a headline catches his attention.

"WEEKLY SHOWCASE.

PRIVATE SHOWING"

Jordan clicks on the link. He grabs his Jack and Coke from the nightstand and takes a sip. He rests against his bed as the video plays. His eyes jump open with shock as he is subjected to a group of young adults. Their heads have been covered with pillowcases. They have been shackled by their hands and feet as if they were cattle. Their nude bodies in full display. Based on the size of their bodies, it can be assumed they are pre-teens and teenagers.

By the shakiness of the camera, he can tell it was a live feed. He'd learned about Red Rooms during his research on the dark web.

Jordan focuses his attention to the message that flashes on the screen.

BIDDING STARTS AT 100 BITCOINS.

PLACE YOUR BIDS NOW.

Overcome with disgust, Jordan shuts down his laptop and throws it to the side. He takes a gulp of his drink and rests his head.

⚘

The next morning, Jordan takes his shower and eats his breakfast. He picks up his phone and dials a number.

"Aye, Bro, you busy right now?"

"No, I'm free until about noon. What's up?"

"I want you to take a look at something real quick. Can you come over?"

"Yea, I will be there in ten."

Jordan opens the door. "What's good, Bro?" He greets his friend, Travis.

"Nothing much, Bro. A day in the life."

"I hear that, man."

"What did you want me to look at?"

"It's right here." Jordan pulls up the page to the video he viewed last night. "I know you are the best at what you do. I need you to hack this address." Travis looks at the website.

"You don't need no hack for this, Bro. I know all about this site. The Hawkes Party been having these weekly showcases for years now."

"Why can't you find this on the regular Internet then? I had to download Tor to find it."

"To hide the location. But it ain't no secret that all this they do in the Mansion. That's why they have it so heavily guarded."

"Speaking of the Mansion...I'm trying to get in there. Any idea how?"

"Like gaining a membership? Or sneaking in?"

"Sneaking in."

"That's a tricky one. There's security all around that place. But I do remember driving by there on my way home one night and no security was around. But this was like two to three in the morning. All the lights were off too."

"Really?"

"Yea, so maybe that's when all the guards call it a night."

"Thanks for the tip, Bro. Good looking."

"Anytime, Bro. Be careful, man. Don't get got."

"You know me, man. I always cover my tracks. I'm like a ghost in these streets." Chuckles.

"Aight, Bro, let me get out of here. Gotta get to lil man's game."

"Tell the fam I said what's up. Soon as I get some time off, I'm coming to see 'em."

♣

13 hours later...

Jordan creeps around the corner of The Hawkes Mansion. Relieved to see it just as Travis has said. He scoured the area for security guards. The street looks clear. He parks his car around the corner. He grabs his utility bag, which is full of bomb detonators. He gets out the car and strolls to the Hawkes Mansion.

Jordan begins his work, lining the outside of the Mansion with the detonators. He gets to the backyard and discovers the door cracked open. Someone must have forgotten to close it. He creeps up to the door and slowly opens it. He lines the area with bomb detonators. Hearing footsteps, he scrambles to find somewhere to hide. He notices a door and slips inside.

Jordan grabs his flashlight from his utility back. He turns it on and observes his area. He jumps in panic as he sees the room decorated in dead bodies, guts, intestines, and blood. He gags as he forces back a scream.

Jordan creeps back to the door he snuck in and peeks out the crack of it. Noticing the lights are out and the door is shut, he lets out a sigh of relief and opens the door. He quietly unlocks the door that leads to the backyard. He panics when he opens the door and an alarm sounds.

He flees through the door and runs to the side of the Mansion. He scrambles to find the remote for the detonators, and he instantly presses the button. He runs as the Mansion blasts into an explosion.

Jordan runs back to his truck and drives to the driveway of the Mansion. He grabs his guns and knives and shove them into their compartments. He gets out the truck and enters the Mansion again to search for the members of the Party. He draws his guns in case some survived the explosion.

When he assures all the members of the party are dead, he begins to collect the bodies and load them in his truck. He jumps in his truck, starts the engine and flees the Mansion before police arrive at the scene.

Donald And The Vultures Home Of Healing

Donald reads his card.

THE EXECUTIONER

VISIT <u>THE VULTURES HOME OF HEALING</u>. ACQUIRE THE FOLLOWING ITEMS: THE HEART OF ROSE BRANCH, THE BRAIN OF STEPHEN KNIGHT, THE TONGUE OF ANTHONY GIVENS, THE EYES OF DANIELLE STEVENS, THE HAND OF GERALD ADAMS, THE FOOT OF KAREN TURK. DELIVER ALL ITEMS HERE.

"That's oddly specific." Donald thought to himself. He puts the card down and grabs his laptop. He pulls up the internet and searches for The Vultures Home Of Healing.

Welcome to The Vultures Home Of Healing.

This is a place where seniors can grow and enhance their skills to a new level. A new way of thinking. A new way of life. The Vultures Way.

The Vultures Home Of Healing formed in the 1900s by original board members Oscar Branch, Doris Knight, Gregory Stevens, Janay Adams, Carlisle Turk, and Heather Givens.

He picks up the card and reads the names again. "What the hell?" He thinks to himself. He returns to the internet and researches the names of the board members.

Oscar Branch (1929 -1989), City Council, Ward 1. Deceased. Death by fire.

Doris Knight (1929 – 1989), City Council, Ward 2. Deceased. Death by fire.

Gregory Stevens (1929 – 1989), City Council, Ward 3. Deceased. Death by fire.

Janay Adams (1929 – 1989), City Council, Ward 4. Deceased. Death by fire.

Carlisle Turk (1929 – 1989), City Council, Ward 5. Deceased. Death by fire.

Heather Givens (1929 – 1989), City Council, Ward 6. Deceased. Death by fire.

He does further research.

"VULTURES HOME OF HEALING

SUSPECTED OF ILLEGAL PRACTICES"

"BOARD MEMBERS OF VULTURES

HOME OF HEALING RUMORED TO

PRACTICING SATANISM"

"TWENTY FATALITIES DISCOVERED

AT THE VULTURES HOME OF

HEALING IN THE PAST SIX

MONTHS"

"A CULT OF SATANISTS ACCUSED

OF SACRIFCING A COUPLE OF

EVANGELISTS"

Donald thinks back to the conversation with Evelyn and Eryn. He turns off his computer and goes to sleep.

♟

The next morning, Donald prepares his suitcase for his venture to The Vultures Home Of Healing. He leaves the house and gets in his car.

He pulls into the parking lot of The Vultures Home Of Healing. He grabs his suitcase and enters the building. He walks to the reception desk.

"Hello. How may I help you?" The receptionist greets him.

"Good morning. My name is George Flank. I called in this morning to do a story on the facility."

"Oh, yes. You're the journalist."

"Yes, ma'am."

"And you are studying at Cleveland State University?"

"Yes." Donald flashes his fake student ID.

"Welcome, Mr. Flank. You already have the clearance from the President. Feel free to look around and take as long as you need."

"Thank you so much."

Donald walks off into the building. He ventures down the hall and peeks in on the different rooms. He looks at the names on his card again. He walks into the room of Rose Branch. Relieved to see she's under heavy sedation, he takes a plastic bag, his gloves, and scalpel out of his suitcase. He puts on his gloves and lifts her robe. He makes an incision around her heart. He lifts the skin and makes another incision. He digs his hands in and pulls out her heart. He places the heart in the plastic bag. He places all the items in his suitcase. He covers up Rose's body and moves on to the next room.

Donald enters the room of Stephen Knight. He quickly gets to work on obtaining his brain. He puts on a new pair of gloves, takes out his scalpel and a new plastic bag. He makes an incision around Stephen's head. He pulls off the skin and makes another incision around the brain. He takes the brain and puts it in the plastic bag. He covers up Stephen's brain and leaves the room.

Donald enters the room of Anthony Givens. He pulls on a fresh pair of gloves. He pulls out a blade and a new plastic bag. He cuts out Anthony's tongue and slips it in the bag. He leaves the room.

He enters the room of Danielle Stevens. He pulls out a fresh pair of gloves, his scalpel and a new plastic bag. He makes an incision around her eyes and gouges out her eyeballs. He places them in the bag. He leaves the room.

He enters the room of Gerald Adams. He pulls out a fresh pair of gloves, his meat cleaver, and a new plastic bag. He stuffs gauzes in Gerald's mouth. He takes the cleaver and whacks at his ankle until his foot gets loose enough to pull off. He takes the foot and places it in the bag.

Donald enters the room of the final patient, Karen Turk. To his surprise, she's awake, reading a book. She looks up at him.

"Hello, Doctor. Is it time for my medicine?" She asks him.

"Um…yes it is."

"I haven't seen you before. Are you new?"

"Yes. I'm filling in for your Doctor." He notices the pills and water on the table. He hands her the pills and the glass of water. Karen takes her pills and drinks the water. She then lies down on her bed.

Donald opens his suitcase and takes out a syringe filled with a poisonous homemade concoction. He eases the syringe in her neck and watches as her body jerks uncontrollably before she eventually gives in to the toxic substance.

Donald quickly puts on a pair of gloves. He takes out his cleaver and a new plastic bag. He chops off Karen's hand and slides it in the bag. He throws all of the items in the suitcase, covers Karen's body, and leaves the room.

"Thank you again for letting me tour the facility today. I have everything I need."

"Our pleasure. Good luck with your classes."

Donald leaves The Vultures Home Of Healing. He throws his suitcase in the trunk. He jumps in his car, starts the engine, and drives off.

Peter And The Shrew's Nest

P eter reads his card.

THE CONDUCTOR

LOCATE AND ABDUCT THE FOLLOWING PEOPLE: MICHAEL HAWK, CRAIG EAGLE, ARNOLD CROW, KENNETH GULL, XAVIER VULTURE. DELIVER THEM HERE ALIVE.

Peter begins his research.

"KENNETH GULL HOLDS RIBBON
CUTTING CEREMONY FOR THE
TEMPLE OF GULLES"

"CRAIG EAGLE UNLEASHES
THE LITTLE EAGLES
SANCTUARY"

"ARNOLD CROW, FOUNDER OF
THE TEMPLE OF CROWES"

"MICHAEL HAWK FORMS THE
HAWKES PARTY"

"XAVIER VULTURE OPENS THE
VULTURES HOME OF HEALING"

Peter does further research.

The Temple Of Gulles formed in the 1900s by original board members Oscar Branch, Doris Knight, Gregory Stevens, Janay Adams, Carlisle Turk, and Heather Givens.

The Little Eagles Sanctuary formed in the 1900s by original board members Oscar Branch, Doris Knight, Gregory Stevens, Janay Adams, Carlisle Turk, and Heather Givens.

The The Temple Of Crowes formed in the 1900s by original board members Oscar Branch, Doris Knight, Gregory Stevens, Janay Adams, Carlisle Turk, and Heather Givens.

The The Hawkes Mansion formed in the 1900s by original board members Oscar Branch, Doris Knight, Gregory Stevens, Janay Adams, Carlisle Turk, and Heather Givens.

The Vultures Home Of Healing formed in the 1900s by original board members Oscar Branch, Doris Knight, Gregory Stevens, Janay Adams, Carlisle Turk, and Heather Givens.

"A CULT OF SATANISTS

ACCUSED OF SACRIFICING

A COUPLE OF EVANGELISTS"

"TEMPLE OF GULLES SUSPECTED

OF DEVIL WORSHIPPING

"BOARD MEMBERS OF THE

LITTLE EAGLES SANCTUARY

BELIEVED TO PRACTICE

SATANIC WORSHIP"

"MEMBERS OF TEMPLE OF

CROWES BELIEVED TO

PRACTICE SATANISM"

"THE HAWKES PARTY BELIEVED

TO ENGAGE IN OCCULT

PRACTICES"

"BOARD MEMBERS OF VULTURES

HOME OF HEALING RUMORED TO

PRACTICING SATANISM"

Peter retires his search and goes to sleep. He's found all he needs to know. Tomorrow begins his journey.

ⵊ

Peter awakes the next morning and prepares his bag. He leaves the house and gets in his truck and drives off. He starts at the Little Eagles

Sanctuary. He pulls into the parking lot and enters the building.

"Hello, ma'am. I was wondering if you knew who this man was?" Peter shows her a picture.

"That's Craig Eagle. He's the founder of Little Eagles Sanctuary."

"Do you know where I can find him?"

"Oh, I don't know. He has never come here once since I started working here over 20 years ago. Some of us even joke if he's still alive."

"Thank you for your time, ma'am." Peter leaves The Little Eagles Sanctuary and drives to The Vultures Home Of Healing. He parks his car and enters the building.

"Good morning, ma'am. I was wondering if you knew this man?"

"Xavier Vulture? Everyone knows he's the founder of The Vultures Home Of Healing."

"Do you know where I can find him?"

"Sorry, I can't help you there. I've never seen him in person. I've only heard about him."

"Thank you for your time."

Peter leaves the building and returns to his car. Confused, he pulls out his phone and does another search. He clicks through the pages and finds a headline that catches his interest.

"1989 FIRE: MYSTERY UNSOLVED. WHAT HAPPENED TO THE OTHERS?"

In October of 1989 there was an explosion that led to the deaths of several people, including City Council members Oscar Branch, Doris Knight, Gregory Stevens, Janay Adams, Carlisle Turk, and Heather Givens.

This following, what is rumored to be the sacrificial ritual of Evangelists Don and Valerie Bobbins to resurrect a dark lord.

Yet, a new discovery has surfaced. During a final investigation of the crime scene, a police officer retrieved new evidence: a tape recorder.

After successful transmission and analysis of the evidence, there is reason to believe that other members were present during that event, but their bodies were never found after the fire.

So, the mystery remains:

What happened to the other bodies?

Peter starts his car and drives to the Downtown Cleveland Public Library. He parks his car and enters the building. He walks to the Special Collections archives. He gets on the computer and pulls up the inter-department search. He searches for the Fire Of 1989.

"WHAT REALLY HAPPENED DURING THE FIRE OF 1989?"

"1989 FIRE: MYSTERY UNSOLVED. WHAT HAPPENED TO THE OTHERS?"

"1989 FIRE: BODIES RUMORED TO BE MISSING"

"1989 FIRE: NEW EVIDENCE SURFACED PRESENTING STARTLING CONCLUSIONS"

The Fire of 1989 caused a lot of chaos, but the smoke still hasn't cleared. New evidence has surfaced presenting a startling conclusion.

Were there more people than were first noted to take part in the sacrificial ritual of Don and Valerie Bobbins? According to the recent transcription of a mysterious tape recorder, new phenomena could be unleashed. Police have yet to reveal the transcription.

One thing is for certain: The Hunt Isn't Over. Stay tuned as we provide the most up-to-date details.

Peter walks away from the computer screen and leaves the library. He returns to his car. He starts the engine and drives to City Hall.

"Yes, sir? Can I help you?" The officer asks Peter as he approaches the desk.

"Hello, officer. I was just wondering if the bodies were ever found from the Fire Of 1989?"

"Excuse me?"

"The Fire Of 1989? The case of Don and Valerie Bobbins? I was just reading some articles about it and there was supposedly a tape recorder discovered at the crime scene."

"Sir, that case was dismissed years ago."

"I'm aware. I was just wondering if the missing bodies were ever found."

"No. It's been an unsolved mystery. After years of trying with no leads, we finally let it go."

"What about the tape recorder? The article says it's been transcribed but was never released publicly."

"Yes, the tape recorder never really amounted to any breakthroughs. Just a bunch of random voices and weird sounds that was more chaotic than anything."

"Is the tape recorder still in possession?"

"Yes it's still in possession. Why?"

"Just wondered why police never released the transmission publicly."

"I just told you why. The analysis did nothing but lead us back to square one. We ran around in circles for years over it. It's over our heads."

"I understand. Thank you for your time, officer." Peter turns to leave the station.

♃

The police officer grabs his cell phone and dials a number.

"Scout here. We have a code black."

♃

Peter reaches for the car door, but he loses his balance as his body falls to the ground, unconscious.

♪

Peter slowly regains consciousness. He squints his eyes to focus. He is in an unknown room. His mouth shut with duct tape. His hands handcuffed. His feet tied with rope. He scours the room. He is confused as to why he is surrounded by 6 unidentified people.

"I bet you're wondering why you're here." A man says to him. "You just couldn't leave it alone. Could you?" Peter tries to talk but his voice is muffled.

"Decades of covering it up and waiting for this shit storm to blow over." Another man says. "Thinking we can finally come out from hiding. Only for some prick to ruin it."

"We've been in this god damn dungeon for too long." A third man says. "We'd be damned if you ruin this for us."

Peter attempts to scream as one of the men walks up to him and knocks him unconscious again. His face is covered with a bag. His limp body is lifted and hurled over the man's shoulders. He is taken to a manhole and tossed inside. The lid to the manhole is replaced, and Peter's body is left to rot.

The Final
Countdown

Evelyn And Eryn Prepares The Altar

Evelyn and Eryn prepare the altar for the missing components. Eryn has already acquired his items, which included fresh blood from a pig, horse, cow, and lamb. He sits the jars of the fresh animal blood around the altar. They embrace each other in their nudity as they wait for the others to arrive.

Charlotte Visits Professor Amari

Charlotte observes the scroll again. She picks up her phone and dials a number.

"Hello, Professor Amari, this is Professor Hortense. I was wondering if you had a moment. I need you to look at something and translate if you can."

"Of course. Anything for you, dear Charlotte."

"You're the best. I will see you soon."

Charlotte grabs the scroll and leaves the house. She jumps into her car and drives to Professor Amari's house.

"Charlotte, how are you? We've missed you at the school today."

"Yes...forgive me I had...some business to take care of. I forgot to call in. I'm so scatterbrain lately."

"No worries. We've all been there. Just wondered if you were well."

"Yes, I am fine. But...I don't have much time right now. Do you think you could translate something for me?"

"Of course. What is it?" Charlotte takes the scroll out of her purse and hands it to him. Professor Amari takes the scroll and reads the text.

Charlotte becomes alert when she notices Professor Amari's expression change.

"Where did you get this?"

"I stumbled across it during research."

"What were you researching?"

"Nothing important. Just something for a class project."

"You know...this is evil. Its not good to dabble into such dark forces. Are you sure everything is alright?"

"Yes, everything is fine. I promise."

"I'm afraid I can be of no help here. This is powers far beyond my abilities."

"I understand. Thank you for your time. I will just leave." Charlotte reaches for the scroll. Professor Amari snatches it away. "Professor Amari?"

"I'm sorry, dear Charlotte. But I am afraid I cannot let you have this."

"But it's mine."

"Not anymore. I'm also afraid I cannot let you leave until you are cleansed of the evil that has possessed you." Charlotte expresses terror as Professor Amari charges toward her with a dagger.

Charlotte scatters to run to the door, but she is blocked by Professor Amari. He grabs her and pins her down to the floor, forcing the dagger toward her. Charlotte struggles against Professor Amari's strength. She knees him in his private area. Professor Amari hurdles over in pain.

Charlotte pushes him off her. She mounts him and bites a chunk of his skin of his cheek. Professor Amari howls in agony as he grabs his face, Charlotte reaches for the dagger and jams it in his chest. She instantly pries the scroll from his hand and flees from the house.

Victor Has A Surprise Visitor

Victor cruises along the street. He jerks and runs off the road as he is attacked by someone from the back seat. One of Father Hector's men, he presumes. Victor loses control of the steering wheel and crashes into a tree as the assailant punctures his skin with a blade. Both men fall unconscious from the impact of the crash.

ℒ

Victor slowly regains consciousness. He panics and snaps his attention to the back seat. The assailant is still passed out. Victor checks his pulse. Nothing. He clenches the blade and rips it out of his side. He rips his shirt to make a bandage to stop the blood. He struggles to get out of the car and drags the assailant's body out of the back seat. He ditches him on the side of the road. He returns to the car and attempts to start the ignition, but to no success.

"Fuck!" He shouts. He gets out the car and walks to the front, lifting the car's hood. The engine is fried. Victor grabs his cellphone and dials a number.

"Hey it's me. I need you to meet me ASAP."

Victor sighs with relief when his friend arrives sooner than expected.

"Man, what happened?" He asks, concerned.

"Long story. Don't have time for it now. I need to borrow your truck. Stay here with the car. I've already called AAA. I have somewhere to be."

"No problem, man."

"Good looking." Victor rushes to the back of his car and opens the trunk. He grabs Father Hector's body and hauls it over his shoulder.

"What the hell is that?" His friend asks, confused.

"No time to explain. Just stay with the car. I will catch up with you later." He throws the body in the trunk of his friend's car. He gets in the driver's seat and drives off.

Donald And The High-Speed Chase

Donald panics as he is surrounded by policemen with their guns drawn. He glances at the time. 10:15 p.m. He inhales and holds his breath for a moment. Visions of his daughter floods into his mind. He grabs the cross that dangles around his neck. He exhales. He slams his foot on the gas pedal and charges through the swarm of police officers. He ducks as they open fire at his car.

Relieved to still be alive, Donald continues to race against traffic. He loses consciousness as his car is hit by a commercial truck, flipping it off the road.

🎭

Donald slowly regains consciousness. He panics as he scours the area for his briefcase. He locates his car and scrambles to run toward it. He rips open the door and grabs his suitcase. He quickly limps from the scene before the police arrive.

Peter Aborts Mission

P eter regains consciousness. He panics when he observes his surroundings. It's dark. It smells like filth. He attempts to move but is restrained. Memories of the recent events that led him to this predicament pops in his mind. He then remembers his mission. Visions of his girlfriend flood his mind.

With his newfound strength, Peter struggles and fights against his restraints to push through. He remembers his pocketknife that he always keeps handy in his sock. He reaches for it and begins to cut at the rope that binds his feet.

When his feet are free, he struggles to make it to the ladder that leads to the surface of the manhole. He clenches the ladder and flips upside down. He repeatedly kicks at the lid of the manhole until it slides open.

Peter stumbles out of the manhole and runs out into traffic, hoping to get someone's attention.

The taxi driver slams his foot on the brakes, as he catches Peter just in time. He jumps out of the car. "What the hell, man?!" He sees Peter needs help and he rushes to his aid. He rips the tape off his mouth.

"DRIVE!" Peter shouts at him as he jumps into the back seat of the car.

The Plot Thickens

Evelyn and Eryn smile as the others rush to the altar. Dawn, Jordan, Kane, and Darryl have already made it ahead of schedule. The altar has been set with the hostages locked in cages.

"Welcome back." Evelyn greets them. "We assume everyone has achieved their tasks?"

"I lost them." Peter says nervously. "They caught me blindsided and tossed me in a sewer. They got away. It was no time left to find them."

"We are very disappointed in you, Peter. Those were going to be some of the sacrifices, but no worries. You all will just have to take their place."

"Excuse me?!" Charlotte snaps.

"Oh, hell no!" Kane barks. "That wasn't part of the terms."

"The terms were to complete your tasks as ordered by the time given. If not, there will be consequences. We never said what those consequences were aside from your family members paying the price."

"You've got to be fucking kidding me!" Jordan lashes out. "Look, man…we've done what you have asked. We completed our mission. Why the hell can't you just take him? Why do we all have to pay for his fuck up?"

"Because we are a team. We are all in this together."

"Man, fuck you!" Dawn shouts. "I ain't ask to be part of this team. I just wanted to complete my mission and be done with you assholes."

"Now you telling us that because *one* person couldn't complete his mission that we're *all* just fucked?" Victor adds.

"Do you know what I had to do to get these items?" Donald snaps.

"You put in the same level of commitment as everyone else."

"Man...Me and Kane ought to waste your punk asses right now!" Jordan threatens.

Eryn presses a button, releasing traps on all of them, binding their hands and feet. They struggle against their restraints.

Eryn takes a bucket. Evelyn presents a dagger. She starts with Jordan. She takes the dagger and slashes his neck. Eryn holds the bucket under his neck as the blood drains. The others fight to break their restraints as Evelyn and Eryn makes their way to each of them.

When they have everyone's blood, Evelyn and Eryn hold hands and they look to the sky as they say the chant.

"Oh dark one...We call upon you now. Rise from the underworld. Take your place among the living."

"Oh dark one...We call upon you now. Rise from the underworld. Take your place among the living."

"Oh dark one...We call upon you now. Rise from the underworld. Take your place among the living."

"Oh dark one...We call upon you now. Rise from the underworld. Take your place among the living."

"Oh, dark one...We call upon you now. Rise from the underworld. Take your place among the living."

They fall silent as they wait for the ritual to take effect. Silence. They wait patiently in the cold, dark forest.

"Why didn't it work?" Evelyn asks Eryn. She grows aggravated.

"Did we say the chant right?"

"Yes. I read it ten times before we started."

"The altar is set right"

"Just as it was in the image."

"What time is it?" She glances at her watch. 12:05 a.m.

"Just after midnight. The time should have been right when we started." She said, confused. "Unless...Peter compromised it all when he failed to complete his mission."

"That doesn't make sense. A sacrifice is a sacrifice regardless of who it is."

"But, remember what the rules of the game stated. You must present the names of your sacrifices prior to starting the ritual. Zettagoryan will come to claim the souls of the names of those we imprint in the book. We already wrote the names of our chosen sacrifices."

"FUCK!" Eryn growled. "I told you we should have chosen people we knew to be the components. But you were so hellbent on these imbeciles."

"Fuck off! Don't act like you weren't sure of them as well. Especially Jordan and Kane. You praised them."

"Wait! You hear that?" Eryn says. Evelyn stops talking and listens in. Anxiety overcomes them as the trees around them begin to rumble and sway violently. They grow paranoid as they hear loud thumps and the ground beneath their feet begin to shake.

Evelyn screams when she and Eryn become trapped in a cage.

"Did you accidently press the button?"

"No, I don't even have the remote. I gave it to you."

They focus their attention when they become surrounded by five mysterious men draped in hooded robes; their faces covered with masks.

"You thought you could outsmart us?" The men taunt them.

"We've planned this all along..."

"We planted the game for you to find..."

"We led you to the other participants..."

"We orchestrated this all...so you can do the work for us."

"And now the time has come to finish what we started 30 years ago."

"Time for you to join your mother and father."

Evelyn and Eryn cry out in terror as the demon charges at them.

Michael Hawk, Craig Eagle, Arnold Crow, Kenneth Gull, and Xavier Vulture disappears from the scene...

Stay Connected

Follow Stacy Cox (StaceMeister0) to be kept up-to-date on all works, including new releases and upcoming books.

Author's Spotlight:
www.lulu.com/spotlight/StacyCoxStaceMeister0

Facebook @StaceMeister0

Twitter @stacemeister0

Instagram @stacemeister0